Sister,

May you experience comfort & peace wherever there is loss.

Much Love,
Sandreka

The Birds & The Bees

BY SANDREKA Y. BROWN

Lagrange GA

THE BIRDS AND THE BEES

Copyright © 2022 by Sandreka Y. Brown All rights reserved.

Printed in the United States of America. No part of this publication may be used or reproduced, stored in a retrieval system, transmitted in any form or by any means-electronic mechanical, photocopy, recording or by any information storage and retrieval system, except for brief quotations in printed reviews, without the prior written permission of the publisher. iSeebookz Publishing LLC Suite 300 Commerce Ave Suite 137B Lagrange Ga 30241

ISBN 979-8-9854863-0-8

Cover Design Y.D. Rowland

Book Design Cheryl Litton

First Edition 2022

10 9 8 7 6 5 4 3 2 1

This is a work of fiction, names, characters, places, events, locales, and incidents are either products of the author's imagination or used in a fictitious manner. Any resemblance to actual persons, living or dead, or actual events is purely coincidental.

The Birds & The Bees

Fighting the Flesh

the Birds & the Bees

I Love Taking a trinket from my mother's *she-cave*. It was the forbidden room as a little girl, and to touch her perfumes, lotions, foundation, lipstick, fingernail polish, and jewelry was a no-no. She told me those items weren't for little girls and would attract the wrong type of attention. She was determined that I would not repeat our family cycle of having children out of wedlock. My mother had my brother Keith at sixteen and forfeited the rest of her childhood. Whenever she thought I was acting beyond my years, my mother would remind me that I had better not come home with a baby and warned that she would put me out of her house if I did. Surprisingly, she allowed me to enter into her fascinating woman's paradise when she did my make-up for my junior prom. The ambiance of her private sanctuary took my breath away.

I stood, eyes widened with my hands covering my mouth, gazing at beauty products, magazines, books, Bibles, personal journals, pens, silky nightgowns, matching undies, and burning candles. She opened the floodgates of womanhood I had not yet experienced, and I enjoyed getting pampered by her. That day in my mother's bathroom sparked my dream of sharing my own sanctuary and creating extra special moments with my own daughter one day. It never occurred to me that I would stand in the same room and flush the most delicate part of that dream away. Thinking back to that day, I remembered as if it was yesterday.

My bladder called a third time and yanked me out of the fog of papers waiting for my signature and the constant calls about schedule changes. I dashed to the employee's restroom. Looking at my reflection in the mirror, I blinked back to the start of my anguish and wondered how I got here. It started with my faulty thinking that I was an exception to the rule when it came to the birds and the bees. I had been stung quite a few times directly by the stinger without the inevitable happening. However, the allergic reactions caused a great scare, but I never swelled up like a balloon. Whatever the reason, I was always relieved. I had imagined pollinating with my husband and not just some random bee.

I dreamt of revealing it to him like a scene I once saw in a movie. He would unwrap an unexpected gift of a onesie that read *World's Best Dad*. Excitement would fill the air with continual hugs

the Birds & the Bees

and kisses while deciding who to tell first...my parents or his. Instead, there I was, knocking on thirty's door and a little embarrassed.

My life had already been mapped out; I was three years behind schedule, to say the least. All the other destinations on my life's map had been stamped by my presence. Yet, despair filled my heart, and there seemed to have been a roadblock to the place I longed to be, called holy matrimony. Unlike the GPS, life didn't automatically reroute me to my desired destination. This deferred dream made my heart sick; sick and tired of hoping and praying. Quite frankly, I had grown tired of being sick and tired. If my hopes came true, great! If it didn't, that was fine too. In the meantime, I had settled for just playing around with one bee. His name was Talin; he was a busy bee who enjoyed eating and mating with this queen bee. There were no expectations to uphold because when it came to marriage, he had been there, done that, and wasn't interested in doing it again.

He had one larva from each of his two previous marriages. He only desired a company bee that didn't include confinement to one hive. So going with the flow, I enjoyed the honey from his honeycomb. Now all of the good-getting had caused an allergic reaction that I hoped was due to work stress.

It had been seven days, and there was still no sign of *Aunt Flow*. Anxious, worried thoughts grew by the day, and instead of enjoying his sweet honey, I couldn't let go of the thought that his venom was catapulting me from a beautiful springtime of my womanhood into motherhood.

The unknown had me breaking out into a sweat, more scared than the town harlot walking into a church during summer revival. Finally, I couldn't take it anymore. Was I pregnant or not?

After returning from the store, I opened the bag and pulled out the home pregnancy test. Using my finger to follow, I read the directions as if I were studying for a test. I was a first-time user, and I didn't want to mess anything up. I chose the second option because I wasn't sure I had five seconds of urine. The sound of heavy rain filled my ears as the cup filled. Submerging the absorbent tip of the test in the urine caused my mind to think back on my submersion in the baptismal water when I was twelve. A new spiritual life began after coming out of that water; now, I couldn't help but wonder if a physical life would come from my own water. I put the rectangular plastic cap back over the absorbent tip and laid it on the bathroom counter as I paced the floor-from my bedroom to the bathroom.

Three minutes felt like three years as my life could drastically be changing. Pacing back and forth, I was too scared to think about anything. Too afraid to even pray because I knew everything was not okay. The timer jarred me from my daze. A tremendous gravitational force of disbelief came upon me and pulled me to my knees. The rules of the game had just changed. Now, there were expectations for my busy bee, but out of fear, he avoided me. There was no excitement; I only carried shame. This place wasn't on my map, and I had just lost my sense of direction.

With the trembling stick in my hand, I remember calling my friend Vea to ease my troubled mind with her unsung story of womanhood. Vea found out at sixteen that the only exception to the rule is the one you create. Her mother did not allow her or any of her siblings to embarrass the good old Reverend Alvin Givens or disgrace the family name. She said she still vividly remembers the day when her mother drove across two states so they wouldn't run into anyone from their church. She recalled the drive being completely quiet on the ride over, and when it was done, her mother said she should never speak of this to anyone. Nobody knew she was pregnant but her Mama. She didn't even tell her boyfriend.

Their little secret was much the same as the birth control pills, she forced Vea to take until she graduated high school. Taking birth control in my family was a sign that you were mating, and my mother had convinced me that mating was for marriage. Vea continued to say that to ease her pain, she began to get stung over and over again by random bees. Vea became hooked on the feeling even though she didn't like most of the bees. When she met her son's father, she fell in love. It was more than a feeling; they shared a commonality of heart, mind, and soul. After two years of dating him, Vea got comfortable as an old shoe with him as she neglected the exceptions she created. They called themselves being careful, but it only took one time to give in to the moment. Vea was furious with herself for being careless.

She was a junior in college and pregnant. Vea said that she could have easily repeated the acts of her sixteen-year-old self, but this was her love child. Of course, her parents were not happy and told her that she needed to confess her faults before the church. Vea refused, so she was not permitted to come home, and for the entire pregnancy, she stayed away at college. Vea's older sister came to visit after the pregnancy and offered to help. Even though "shacking up" was also a sin to her family, she moved in with her son's father since he had graduated and moved off-campus.

My thoughts were astounded, but Vea had always kept it real with me. After sharing her story, she helped me navigate through my current situation. "God doesn't make mistakes," she said. Deep

the Birds & the Bees

down within myself, I knew that He didn't, but boy did I feel like I just did. "Motherhood is a blessing," she continued, "And I think you would make a great mother." I couldn't fathom raising a child alone like her. Unfortunately, she and her son's father broke up less than a year after her son's birth. My strength to carry out this task could not be compared to her mighty power to raise a boy child all by herself. "Consider all the wonderful people who would love to raise your child if you don't think you can do it." She helped me consider all options as she often thought about other routes she could have taken.

Thought after thought, my mind continued racing, I found myself comparing my situation to Vea's. I was secretly grateful that I was sheltered. In my childish thinking, my parents' more lenient approach with my brother Keith made him seem like their favorite child. It still does, especially when my mother pleaded with me to come to Sunday dinner since Keith and his family had driven up from Columbus. I was just over for Easter two Sundays ago, but Keith spent Easter with his in-laws. It might as well have been Easter again because when Keith came to visit, Mother prepared a spread of his favorite foods... fried chicken, cabbage, collard greens, cornbread, black-eyed peas, fried okra, macaroni and cheese, potato salad, banana pudding, and a pound cake. We played games with the kids, watched sports, and laughed and reminisced about our favorite family memories. Keith always had to bring up when my Jheri curl dried up in elementary school, and I walked around with my hoodie on all day. He was a mean big brother because when we got off the school bus, he snatched my hoodie off and ran towards the house. My brother was the ultimate practical joker, but I learned from the best and got him back when I sent him a fake Valentine's Day candy gram from Janelle Evans. He had a massive crush on her in the seventh grade. He was so embarrassed when he thanked Janelle for the gift, and she told him that it wasn't from her. We can laugh about those memories now, but they weren't funny then.

Having a boyfriend in the seventh grade was not an option for me, but that's when I started to have feelings for boys. In the summer of our seventh-grade year, Nate gave me my first kiss behind my grandmother's shed. His long arms, which he used to dunk basketballs during gym class, wrapped around my waist. I pushed my toes into the ground as he laid a wet one on me. Five seconds later, I ran back to the front of the yard to play. I wanted to spare my butt the whooping I would have received if an adult caught me being fast. My parents were religious, so we went to church every Sunday. My favorite Sunday ritual was Sunday school. There I played teacher's pet to the sweetest person in the world, Mrs. Goodsell. When I got promoted to the teenager's class, Mrs. Goodsell reminded me of the perils of sin and that I should flee youthful lust. Running away from Nate was about more than a good-ole fashioned touch of the rod, it was the thought of what could have happened next.

My mother found a condom in my drawer when I was fourteen. Then, with invisible smoke blowing from her two nostrils while glaring at me with blood-stained eyes that pierced my soul, she asked, "What's this?" My mouth was moving, but no words came out. It wasn't what it looked like. Honestly, I got it from a boy named Ricardo, who was giving them out in class. I took one, not wanting to be shamed as a goodie two shoes. I should have known better than to put it in my drawer; now, my mother has it. "So, you are having sex now?" My mother continued to ask me question after question.

Tears trickled down my face as I began to at least answer my mother's questions. "A boy at school gave it to me; I didn't know what to do with it. I swear, Mama!" "You what?" Mother yelled. She didn't like me to use the word swear. "I meant I promise Mama. I'm telling you the truth." Mother still whooped my butt that night and accused me of doing what she said was designed for married people. The rest of the night, I suffered more pain from disappointing her than the ten licks to my backside. My mother succeeded in putting the fear of God in me, and that fear still haunts me as I vowed from that day to never disappoint her again.

Seven weeks had passed since talking to Vea, and I still didn't know what to do. I couldn't keep ignoring the life growing inside of me. My fun time had indeed moved me into a different season that tested my beliefs. I didn't condone abortions, but I suddenly found myself in the waiting room of final decisions. Remi Hutson was called three times, but I couldn't move. Uncertainty had not let go of its hold on me, so I decided not to make a choice that day.

The next day I decided to work late to keep my mind busy and off the obvious. Uncertain if it was the stress or just being pregnant, I frequently visited the toilet more that day than ever. This was the third time, and when I turned to grab the tissue and unbutton my pants, I smothered a scream as I stared at the blood that filled the toilet. Panicked, the first person I called was Vea, who gave me the news that I no longer had to decide what to do. I should be relieved, maybe even grateful. Right? No more despising shame, no more thoughts of inadequacy, but the tears that followed didn't deliver relief or joy. The choice inadvertently had been made, and unfortunately, it robbed me of the power to choose.

Grabbing my keys and purse, I left work after speaking with Vea then called the person I feared disappointing the most. Vea begged me not to stay alone that night. She had moved 2,000 miles away after accepting her new position as Dean of Public Health at Gordon University. She knew I desired the love and acceptance of my mother and somehow believed that she would give me just that. "Remi, you have exceeded your mother's expectations and created a great life for yourself. Our parents did their best to steer us in the right direction. I'm not saying everything they say or do is right, but I do know they love us." Vea spoke nothing but the truth, and it was time I faced my fear of rejection, and I prayed my mother would love me through my mess.

Nearly hanging up the phone, anticipating that the voicemail greeting would silence the rings, Mother answered just before I could press the end call button.

"Hello," Mother answered the phone with shortness of breath. She probably was looking all over the house for her cellphone. She misplaces it a lot.

"Hey, Mom." She could hear the tears through my voice.

"What's wrong, honey? Is everything alright?"

I hadn't strategized how to tell her, but for an unknown reason, I asked her, "Mom, have you ever had a miscarriage?"

Without hesitation, she answered, "Yes."

To my knowledge, she had Keith at sixteen, married my dad at nineteen, and had me at twenty. When did she have a miscarriage? Was this a divine intervention to help me gain empathy?

"I think I am having one now."

"Huh, I didn't know you were pregnant."

Her tone alluded that her eyes had widened while her right hand was placed over her heart.

"I'm sorry, Mom. I was processing it myself and needed time to figure things out."

"Oh, honey. I am sorry."

Like being released from several years in prison, I felt free at last. Fear had been replaced with friendship as I began to share from a confused state of being.

"I am not even sure I was ready to be a mother, and the baby's father doesn't want any more kids."

"It's not his choice," my mother said. "You are an adult and capable of taking care of your own child, and you have our support!"

"Remi, are you still there?"

Wetness filled my eyes as frustrated tears had silenced my words, and I wished I had told Mama from the very beginning.

"Uh, huh."

"Baby, come over here tonight. You don't need to be alone."

"I'm headed that way," I said without a thought.

My mother met me at the door with a warm embrace after waving hello before I got out of the car. She must have known that I wouldn't be in the mood to talk. I walked into the house, and we went straight to her room. I flopped down on her bed. I could feel her eyes piercing my back as she held speaking her ordinary words anytime we lay on her bed. I was under a unique circumstance and took full advantage of it.

"Baby, you get some rest. I am going to the store to pick up groceries to cook your favorite meal."

I nodded my head up and down to let her know I heard her.

"I have some hot tea on the dresser for you. Drink it to help you relax."

Words seemed to have left me, and all I could do was shake my head.

Immediately after my mother left her room, my bladder called again. But this usage was different than before as something more than urine came out of me. Suddenly, a river of tears rushed out, watching my child float in water like a withered, lifeless leaf in a sullied puddle of mud. My child, my baby in a final cold, bloody, unsanitary resting place. I prayed that the heartbeat had long since stopped, and my baby couldn't feel the cold or smell the stench or sense that I was far above and not holding him.

That was two years ago, but I'll never forget the day I closed the casket of my offspring by pushing the handle. It might as well have been me burying him six feet under. Yet, there were no ashes to ashes, no dust to dust. There was no dirt to cover him, just my silent prayer, and I prayed that was enough. It's crazy how the simple act of using the bathroom prompts fresh tears and reminds me of the constant fight I have with my flesh.

Batteries not Included

As Soon As I got my weeping under control, I sat on the bed with a glass of wine and called Vea.

"Hey, girl."

I sang out a sad, "Hey."

"What's going on? You don't quite sound like yourself?" After two years, I told Vea how I couldn't believe that I would still be revisiting those thoughts. Was I distraught because of the miscarriage or because the opportunity of love, marriage, and the baby carriage seemed slim to none in this modern-day journey of love and relationship? My conversation with Vea went from my memories of August 15th to how extremely hard I found it to fulfill my faith demands. Sure, it might be easier to remain abstinent if I had never been burned before, but it seemed the older I got, the hotter the fire got. It didn't make it any better to see the people who told you to not play around with fire sitting in the church house booed up with their spouses. Literally, booed up! Believe me, I am not hating, but there seems to be no consideration for those of us whose flesh wants what it cannot have in the house of the Lord. I prayed many prayers and read many books in an effort to fight the flesh, but how long does one have to wait. Was it ever God's plan for one to be sexually untouched well into adulthood?

I can recall seeing my gynecologist because days nine through fourteen were a bit too much to handle. It was a force to be reckoned with. I remember being so on fire that I began to curse at everything: my socks, car keys, TV, dog, and cellphone. Everything around me got on my damn nerves. My doctor gave me some prescribed medication to balance the hormones, but she didn't have the proper water to put this fire out. I know it is written that it is better to marry than burn, but I am not just trying to marry to put out the fire. I know of too many situations where married couples have lost their passion. Even in the religious community, the percentage of divorce is rising. Besides, my candidates for marriage partners have not been good anyway.

"I hear you, Sis. It can be a real fight with your flesh, but it is totally worth it." Vea empathically responded.

"What do you mean? Are you not tempted? How do you do it?" I couldn't help but wonder how she managed so much self-control because she had always been a bee magnet. Vea was just a few years older than me, a single mother, and very attractive by anyone's standards. Was she praying harder, or had her convictions become more tolerable? Having talked the majority of our conversation on the phone, I yielded my listening ear to Vea.

"Girl, I have had enough for an entire lifetime." I chuckled, but Vea did not laugh.

"You know my life hasn't been a pretty picture. After moving in with my son's father, we grew more distant by the day. He worked about eighty hours a week, but I still had to have it. Believe it or not, it was so easy to get. I don't think he ever found out that I was cheating, but as soon as I graduated, he decided to move back home to Maryland, and without a job and waiting for the court to determine child support, I had to move back home too.

My parents had evolved enough that I only had to repent to them and, of course, God. Being a single parent, I knew that I had to do things differently for my son. I thought it was important that I raise him in the church with the same principles I was raised with, even though I had wandered from the faith. But like the prodigal son, I had returned home, and I promised God to wait until I was married. My life became all about my son, and even though I wanted to date, most men disappeared after I told them I was celibate. I genuinely think because I had a son, they saw me as accessible. It has been ten years now; I haven't had relations."

"Omg!!! How do you stay so strong?" I shouted in disbelief.

"Well, let's just say batteries are not included."

"Really!?!"

"Girl, that's your problem. You need to learn how to take care of yourself."

"It's not the same, Vea. I have never been into toys. I prefer the real deal."

"Me too, but this keeps me from bursting at the seam over every Tom, Dick, and Harry, plus it keeps me sin-free."

"So, you're telling me that masturbation is not a sin?"

"Nope! I can't find it anywhere in the Bible. I don't have to worry about getting pregnant, and my needs are being met. I'm telling you, girl, the right vibrator in the right spot will get you there."

Maybe Vea was right because I had to find a way to tame this fire. So, my inquiring mind asked what kind I needed to get. It was worth a try, and I tried it as soon as it came in. It was funny how a battery-powered object could produce real moans, but it didn't deliver the honey. I had to call Vea and let her know this was not working for me.

"Hey, girl, hey!"

"Hey! That package came in."

"Have you put it to use?"

"Yeah, but it didn't get me there."

"What do you mean? Did you have it in the right spot?"

"Of course I did! I know my body."

"Maybe you need to try a different kind?"

"Nah, sis! I want intimacy, and a toy just can't give me that."

"But it can keep you out of hell."

"That's not funny."

"Seriously, I am determined to wait until marriage. I owe that to God for the mess that I have made. Sometimes I wonder if that is why I haven't found anyone yet. Maybe he is punishing me for all the wrong I have done."

"God is not like that, Vea. You are forgiven, and he has afforded new grace to you. You are a wonderful mother and a good catch for any man. I believe it is going to happen for you."

"Maybe Remi, but I am not putting my energy in those hopes. I have six more years before my son is out of the house, and that is my only focus now."

"So, do you actually think you can wait until marriage?"

"Honestly, I really don't know since I haven't been tested, but that is my plan."

"I hear ya...all I know is I'm not wasting my money on any more batteries!"

This made both of us laugh hysterically until a beep interrupted our good time.

"Girl, hold on, I got another call coming in."

Doing His Business

I removed the phone from my ear to see who was calling.

"Hey Vea, let me call you back. My Aunt Cindy is calling on my other line."

"Sure, go ahead."

"I will call you back tomorrow, but I appreciate your transparency."

"Anytime. I love you, sis."

"Love you too."

"Hey, Aunt Cindy," I said as I rushed to answer her call before it stopped ringing. Aunt Cindy was my mother's sister. Mama was the third born of ten children, and Aunt Cindy was the baby of them all. She was eight years older than me, so Aunt Cindy was my babysitter and playmate at times. Aunt Cindy was the first of my mother's siblings to graduate from college. She was our hometown hoop star, and I remember going to her high school and college games. She married Joseph Cunningham, from the men's basketball team, right after they graduated college and immediately started their family.

"Hey, my favorite niece! How are you doing?"

"I'm okay."

"I thought you were going to stop by the other day."

"I totally forgot. I had some things on my mind."

"Are you okay, sweetie? Want to talk about it?"

I released a heavy sigh as I was unsure if I wanted to talk to my Auntie about fighting my flesh or using the batteries to help fight it. How could she understand? She and Uncle Jo have been married for over twenty years.

"I'm okay, Auntie."

"Are you sure, niece? It sounds like something is heavy on your heart."

"I mean... never mind."

The sound of nothingness filled the space between me and Aunt Cindy. I guess she decided to play the waiting game, which reminded me of Mrs. Hill's math class. I hated it when she called on me and would wait in dead silence until I responded.

"Well, I have been trying to find peace in this fight with my flesh. There has to be an exception to the rule because I do not think God intended for me to be thirty-five, husbandless, and engaged in guilty pleasures."

Auntie Cindy burst out laughing at the dramatics in my voice.

"I'm serious!"

"I know you are, and I understand your frustration. You know things have changed a lot from your grandmother's generation to your mother's generation, even mine to yours. Cycles came more around thirteen or fourteen, and now girls are getting a cycle as young as ten. In Grandma Mae's generation, they were getting married anywhere between twelve and fifteen years old. After the man got a job, he soon chose a wife. Many people got married right after graduating high school during your mother's time. In my era, marriage was the thing to do after graduating from college. Nowadays, I am seeing people getting married later in life or not at all."

"Auntie, I know, right! So how are we supposed to remain pure for these many years?"

"Baby girl, listen to me. In life, you just got to do the best you can. God knows your heart, and his love covers a multitude of sins. But listen to me; I need you to keep growing and being the best version of you. Don't let your flesh set your wedding date."

"What do you mean, Auntie?"

"I was a virgin when I met your uncle. We dated two years in college, and I made him wait until marriage. Don't get me wrong, I wanted to, but I thought if he got the milk for free, then he would never marry me."

"He married you, so it worked, right?"

"Wrong! Sweetheart, listen. I don't believe we should be out here sleeping with every man we meet, but I also don't think we should dangle sex as a prize. At the very beginning of our marriage, your uncle and I made good love. We have four amazing kids, and they are the glue keeping us married. Unfortunately, your uncle has broken my heart so many times by being inconsiderate, disrespectful, and sometimes heartless that love-making now lacks love. I just let him do his business. Because I wanted to be married so badly, I overlooked his character. I was more concerned about him wanting the "milk" instead of the whole "cow.""

"Wow! Auntie, I am sorry. I didn't know."

"I am going to be alright. I just don't want you to make the same mistakes. Remi, focus your attention on having a healthy relationship. Get to know your future mate. If you engage in relations, don't let it blind you from who he really is. Follow your own convictions. Some people are using the Bible to stay in unhealthy marriages. Big Mama stayed with Papa Dexter because she did not believe in divorce. All he felt he had to do was protect and provide for her, and she couldn't question the rest. Now, when I look at my marriage, I have fallen into that same cycle. Your uncle is a great protector and provider for our family, and I have only known him. He was my first, and we have been together for twenty-five years. But I can't lie. I have contemplated divorcing him once all the children are out of the house."

"This makes me sad, Auntie."

"Remi, don't be sad for me. I am learning a valuable lesson and growing in the process. However, I wish someone would have told me better, so I am sharing this with you. One of the saddest things is being in a marriage and having to buy batteries."

I burst out laughing as I asked, "You too?" I was thinking about my friend Vea and not me.

"Yep! You know batteries are not included."

"I guess that is better than getting it elsewhere, huh?"

"Yep! I will use it right afterward."

"You are so silly, Auntie Cindy."

I was laughing at my aunt, but she really made sense to me. I want a man to love all of me. I want an enjoyable marriage. I tried to tell Auntie Cindy to just leave. She is a brilliant and attractive woman. She could hold her own, but just like she let me make my own decisions, I have to allow her to make hers.

I looked at the clock and suddenly remembered I had a dinner date scheduled with my crazy, sexy, cool soror Aja. I had forty minutes to get ready.

"Hey, Auntie! I have to meet my friend Aja in a few. Can I come over tomorrow after church?"

"Of course! I am making chicken dressing and collards. Haven't decided on the meat yet."

"I will definitely be there. Love you, Auntie."

"Love you, niece."

Don't Hate the Game

the Birds & the Bees

I Was Out the door in thirty minutes. That was the fastest I ever got ready. So glad the restaurant wasn't too far from me, and I would definitely be getting valet parking tonight. I haven't entirely broken these heels in, and my feet were already hurting. I guess I can fake a smile from the door to our table and back to the car.

I made it a few minutes early, so I texted Aja to see if she had arrived. As usual, she had already gotten the party started with a few drinks at our table. In addition, she texted the directions to our table, so I didn't need the hostess's assistance. As I approached our booth, Aja started boosting my head as usual.

"Come through, PYT!!!!!! You look good, and where did that ass come from."

These high-waisted dressy black joggers did make my butt look good. If anybody was going to let me know, it was definitely Aja. Her line name was No-Filter, and it fit her to the tee. Aja was a Jersey girl who stayed in the South after we graduated from Atlanta's most prestigious historically black women's college. We were as different as night and day, but blood couldn't make us closer than we already were. Aja was confident, vocal, and so much fun. I never heard Aja speak badly about herself. She would also shift the conversation whenever I beat myself up over gaining weight or playing the fool for love. She reminded me of all my admirable attributes that I often fail to celebrate about myself. Aja is thirty-five, single, and childless, just like me. Unlike me, though, it doesn't seem to affect her the same way. She is living her best life, and I love it.

Trying not to blush from her compliment, I responded, "Girl, you know I am the squat queen."

You can know you look good, but a compliment causes happiness to explode from your heart.

"Keep it up, soror. You are gonna be turning heads on our Miami trip."

"You will too, Aja. You look great."

"Thanks! I have been drinking detox tea. You know I hate to sweat unless..."

"Girl, you are crazy."

"I am serious."

"Hi, ladies!"

We both looked to see our favorite waitress. "Hey, Keri," we spoke in unison. We meet here once a week for dinner, and we always request Keri. She is the best waitress ever. "Will it be your usual this week?"

"Yes," Aja said, and I nodded to confirm.

"Great, I will put your orders in and bring you all two glasses of our cabernet brand."

"Thank you, Keri."

Being glad that Kerri had walked off, I couldn't hardly wait to get back on the topic. Aja was undeniably honest and lived in her truth. I knew she would spill the beans if I inquired.

"So....back to your exercise regimen."

"Honey, let me tell you. I exercise one time a week."

"With who?"

"Here's a hint.... One call, that's all."

Looking confused, I said, "Ken Nugent."

"Girl, no! Ken Summers."

"Wait...the guy in your dentistry program?"

"Yes!!!! Don't hate the game, sis."

Was I looking judgmental? I probably was because I never could keep a poker face.

"So, are you all dating?"

"Girl, no! I will never date him. He is so boring."

"So, he's just for a good time?"

"Yes, just a maintenance man to keep everything working until the real thing comes along."

"And what happens when the real thing comes along?"

There were a few moments of silence as Keri brought out our food and drinks.

"How does everything look, ladies?"

"Great!"

"Here are some extra condiments. I will be back to check on you in a few."

"Thank you!" I anxiously said as I eagerly wanted to hear more from Aja.

After we blessed our food, Aja dove into her

dinner. I let her take a few bites, but she would have to multi-task tonight.

"Again, what happens if you start dating someone for real?"

"Look! I think it is good to have someone like Ken, who takes the edge off. That way, I can really get to know someone I am truly interested in without giving it up to him. But, of course, if things get more serious, then I will cut it off with Ken."

"Wait, just like that?"

"Yeah, Ken and I have a mutual understanding."

"So, why don't you just self-pleasure?"

"Honey, I am not wasting my money on batteries when I can have the real deal without the heartache."

"So, Aja, are you saying that you are going to wait until marriage with the guy you will seriously date?"

"Hell no!! All I am saying is that a lot of times, sex clouds our judgment when trying to get to know someone. If my hormones are not raging since I am being taken care of elsewhere, I can take my time and truly get to know him. But, on the other hand, if we become exclusive after spending some months together, I will drop Ken in a heartbeat and only give up to him."

"Wow! You have this all mapped out, huh?"

"I'm just saying. Sex is a natural thing, and it is good for us. Ken and I are consenting adults who have an understanding. I am not going to lie to myself and say I can wait until marriage. It is just a part of the process when dating for some time. I know women who were virgins when they got married, and these heifers are calling me for sexual advice. You remember Dee Dee?"

"Yeah, she crossed a year before us."

"That's her. She married Taj. She bragged about being a virgin, but William told me that Taj told him that sex in his marriage was boring."

"Stop lying. Do you really believe William? He used to gossip too much for me when we all hung out during undergrad."

"I know he isn't lying because Dee Dee called me to get advice. She said it had been drilled into her that sex was nasty all of her life, and it was hard for her to open up and try things with her husband."

"No way!"

"Yes, she also said that she feels like Taj had more fun before her."

"I am speechless."

"All I am saying is I love Jesus, and I love sex too. I am not saying that I am right or wrong in my dealings, but this is where I am."

"I hear you, girl."

"One thing is for sure; I refuse to have a sexless or unenjoyable life."

I sat there in deep thought. I knew Aja wasn't celibate, but this girl was on another level. And poor Dee Dee. It sounds like Taj was "doing his business," as Aunt Cindy named it. There has to be a balance in this. I didn't want to get married for just sex; I wanted to be naked and unashamed with a man who loved and desired all of me.

"One check or two?" Keri interrupted my deep thoughts.

"One check," I heard Aja say.

"Sis, thank you! I got you next week."

"For sure!"

After paying, Aja and I walked to the front to wait for our cars. Even though we have completely different philosophies on living single, I respected Aja's realness. As a matter of fact, I had become Aja while dealing with Talin. But secretly, I wanted more with him. I saw how good a father he was to his two sons, and I wanted that with him and our child. We had grown to be good friends, and I would have never guessed that he would leave me packing when he found out I was pregnant. I never told him about the miscarriage. If he didn't want anything to do with our baby, then he didn't want anything to do with me. Now, I wish I could figure out my truth and just live in it like Aja to live my best life.

"Alright, sis! Same time next week." Aja's car was brought up first.

"I will be here." I waved at her as she drove off and then waited for my car.

Loopholes

I Couldn't Really sleep last night. I tossed and turned as I thought about my conversations with Vea, Aunt Cindy, and Aja. Even though I felt restless, I knew I had to get up and go to church. I told Toi I would meet her there for the 11 o'clock service. If I was a minute late, we would have to sit in the overflow area, and I wanted to be in the sanctuary for the live praise and worship.

I grabbed my phone and texted Toi that I would see her shortly and meet her at our usual seats. Toi and I were definitely creatures of habit because we sat in the same row every Sunday, and if someone took our seats, we would be slightly upset.

I am not going today. Toi texted back.

Are you sick? Is everything okay? I waited for thirty minutes. She still hadn't responded. *Toi, are you okay?*

She immediately texted back. *Sorry girl, go without*

me today. Call me after church.

Toi, I am on my way over. I am your friend, and I am here for you.

Okay, she replied with a crying emoji.

I got up, showered, and threw on my yoga pants. I had no idea what was wrong with Toi. I have only known her for a year. We met at church during a singles' ministry event. There were only a handful of men there compared to the hundreds of women. Toi is the pastor's daughter, but she was a grown woman. She had a great career and bought her own home at thirty. I considered her my lil sis since I was five years older, and I knew something was really wrong. It wasn't like her to miss church.

Traffic downtown was light. It only took me twenty minutes to get to Toi's condo. I called her from the gate, and she buzzed me in and then texted me that her door would be open. I walked into a mess of dishes overflowing in the sink and clothes littering the living space. I was sure a skunk was hiding as the trash smelled extremely bad. This was not like Toi. I always thought she was OCD considering how clean she kept her place. I stepped over the mess and proceeded to her bedroom. She laid there with the covers pulled over her face in complete silence. No TV. No music. Just dead silence.

"Hey, Toi."

She threw up her hand to wave hi as she tossed the cover backward.

"Tell me what's going on."

Tears flowed from her eyes as she sat up against her headboard and wiped her face. "Promise you are not going to judge me or say anything to anyone."

"I promise, and I can't judge anybody."

"Yeah, I know you won't."

"So, what is it?"

"I went last week for my yearly pap smear. Well, my doctor called Friday and told me that I had Gonorrhea."

"Really?"

There were a few moments of silence before I inquired more. It just didn't make any sense. "Toi, I thought you were a virgin."

"I am."

"Help me understand how you caught an STD then."

"I performed oral on Stanley."

"Okay, let's back up. Is it curable?"

"Yes, I picked up the antibiotics yesterday, and I have to go back to the doctor in two weeks to get retested."

"Okay, that is good news."

"Yeah, I am grateful. I never really thought about it. Stanley and I have been seeing each other for a few months, and I thought we were committed to each other. I thought he was okay with us not having sex. He knew I was a virgin. I told him about the pinky promise I made with my dad and God that I would wait until marriage. I didn't know at sixteen that I would be thirty and still single."

"Try thirty-five."

"I can't imagine being your age and not married."

"Wait a minute! What are you saying?"

Toi finally showed another emotion and laughed. "I don't mean it like that."

"I'm listening."

"I'm just saying I would have broken my vow if I had to wait that long."

"Believe me, the struggle is real, and it seems like most of us are trying to find a loophole that doesn't convict us."

In our brief moment of silence, I still couldn't stop thinking why she thought oral sex wasn't sex. I am not sure if she would answer me, but I had questions about her ideology. Before I could frame my questions, Toi blurted out, "I told God that I am trying my best to wait."

Feeling like she just opened the door for me to start my investigation, I asked, "May I ask you a personal question?"

"Sure!"

"Have you ever had an orgasm?"

"Yes, why do you ask?"

"Because you are not technically a virgin anymore."

"I haven't had intercourse!"

"Oral sex is just another form of sex, Toi."

"I mean, I know, but the Bible only says fornication is a sin."

"Okay, let's be real. Sex is sex, but if that clears your conscience, so be it. You know I am not judging. On the other hand, Toi, you have to be smart. At least with intercourse, you can protect yourself."

"I mean...Since I was eighteen, I have been doing this, and I'm just now catching something. At least I can't get pregnant, and my husband can be my first."

I was the last person to judge another, but this was even more mind-blowing than Aja's perspective on sex. Is this what our Christian walk has come to; finding loopholes to appease the flesh while viewing marriage as a scapegoat. I wanted to tell Toi that her loophole was not really a loophole, but then I would have to tell Vea that her toys weren't a loophole. So instead, I just decided to be there for Toi until it was time to go to my aunt's house.

Overcomer

It was 3 o'clock, and the food wasn't quite ready. I was starving because I didn't get a chance to eat breakfast. Toi had me so scared that I barely took a shower before going to check on her. I am glad her situation is curable. Because now, there are some diseases that you can't get rid of.

"Cousin!!!!"

My cousin Shay is here. She is ten years younger than me, but we were really close growing up. I used to babysit her when I was in high school. She is my Aunt Cindy's oldest child. She got married about three years ago and moved to DC. I had no idea that she was home.

"Shay!!! It is so good to see you. I didn't know you were home."

"Girl, I'm just here for a hot second. Lorenzo had a work event in Atlanta, and I decided to come along so I could see the family and get some of Mama's good southern cooking."

"Okay!!!! I live forty minutes away, and I had to get some of your mom's cooking."

"How is Auntie Freda, Remi?"

"My mom is doing good. I was over there two days ago."

I couldn't help but think about how I left Mama's house. They all think I am moody anyway and probably didn't give much thought to me leaving so abruptly. I kissed Mama before leaving and told her that something had come up, and I needed to run. I knew she read right through me, but Mama never did pry. She doesn't ask questions or tries to keep tabs on my life, but she always listens when I can't hold things in anymore. Maybe I should check in with her today and let her know what has been on my mind.

"That's good to hear. Please tell Aunt Freda I said hello."

"Now cuz, you know you better call her. She is going to be upset to know you were here and didn't call."

"You're right! I better call before I leave."

We walked out onto the patio with some fresh lemonade while waiting for the food to be done.

"Hey, cuz! Can I ask you a personal question?"

"Of course! Anything."

"Were you a virgin when you married Lorenzo?"

Shay was just like Auntie Cindy. She didn't mind being honest with you and didn't get easily offended. Shay was a "classy, keep it real" type of woman. She was young yet so wise. She reminded me so much of myself. How did we make it through college virgins? And the temptations were not any easier being at an all-girls college. The opportunities were always knocking on our door. Shay went to a division one school and became very active. She was the president of the Baptist student group for two years. After college, Shay moved to DC, worked for the government, and got involved in a local church. She met Lorenzo at a work event, and they hit it off quickly.

"I was a virgin when I met Lorenzo, but we didn't make it until marriage."

"Do you regret it, or do you think it clouded your vision?"

Shay must have seen it in my eyes that I really needed someone to talk to. She didn't ask me where this was coming from or anything. "Not at all. Lorenzo and I have always been on the same page. He knew I was a virgin, and he actually wanted to wait. One night, we had some drinks, and one thing led to another."

"So, are you blaming it on the alcohol?" I sang out.

With her hand trying to catch the lemonade falling from her laughing mouth, she replied, "No!"

After the laughing subsided, she elaborated more. "I did it because I wanted to. I knew I had met my husband. I told God that I would wait for my husband, and I did. Now, Lorenzo suggested that we go back to waiting after that one time because he knew my convictions were strong. So, we didn't do it again until our honeymoon night."

"That's beautiful."

"He is something special, Cuz."

"So, how is married life?"

"I love it! Marriage is beautiful, but it takes work like any other relationship. It is a constant pursuit of each other and communicating effectively. Lorenzo is my best friend and partner for life. He is very supportive of my goals, and I support his dreams and goals too."

"Now, that is the best thing I have heard all weekend."

"Hey, Cuz. Your time is coming."

Auntie Cindy yelled out that dinner was ready. We got up and headed toward the back door.

"Did Auntie make macaroni and cheese?" I changed the subject before entering the house to

the Birds & the Bees

get us back in our laughing mood.

"Yes, ma'am. I went to the store this morning and bought the ingredients. I was not going back to DC without eating some."

Before entering the door, I gave Shay a big hug as she was what I called an overcomer.

A Mother's Child

On The Drive over to my parent's house, I couldn't stop thinking about how transparent Auntie Cindy and Shay were. I am sure their transparency with me is just a mere reflection of their communication with each other. Then I started thinking about the breakthrough moment with my mother after Vea strongly suggested that I should call her when I had a miscarriage.

I guess the current realities of that day kept me from exploring our shared experience. But deep within, I had a notion that documenting her story would somehow give me peace to live out my very own. When I made it to the house, my mother, already in her nightgown, was sitting on her ottoman watching the movie network. This was her Sunday evening ritual after cooking and cleaning.

"Hey, Mother!" I let myself in and knew just where to find her.

"Hey there." She was just as surprised as I was to find me visiting on a Sunday evening. "Were you in the neighborhood?"

"Not too far. Shay made a quick trip home, and Auntie Cindy invited me over for dinner."

"Shay's home and she hasn't come to see me?"

"Shay told me that she was going to give you a call. She flew down with Lorenzo for a business meeting."

"Those two are always on the go."

My eyes were fixed on the TV, but I kept contemplating how to initiate the conversation. Should I start with Mama or me? Should I start with the questions? Should I wait until the movie goes off? Then, seizing the moment, I went forth as a sharpshooter, just like when I told her about my miscarriage.

"Hey, Mom."

"Uh, huh." Her eyes had become glued to the TV.

"What did Grandma teach you about the birds and the bees?"

Her shoulders started to quickly move up and down as she began to laugh out loud, "Nothing."

"Your Auntie Paige told me about birth control pills," she said. Auntie Paige was the oldest sister.

"I don't remember Mama even teaching me about menstrual cycles."

Becoming curious, I asked, "How did you learn how to care for yourself?"

"I think it was health class...yeah, it was an all-girls health class."

Things were becoming more apparent, and I began to understand why. I couldn't stop here. I wanted to know more.

"Was she disappointed with you when you had a baby at sixteen?"

"If she was, she never said it. At my age, she was already married to your grandpa."

"Oh, wow!"

"Yeah, she was married at thirteen."

The spirit of talking must have fallen on Mom because she began to tell me more than what I requested. "Now, your father's mother, Grandma Evelyn, was quite the opposite. They swear I got pregnant to destroy your father's collegiate future and reputation in the church. After Keith was born, your father dropped out of college and provided a place for us. She told him that he had disgraced the family and couldn't come back and live there."

That was the same scare tactic she used with me. The nerve of her! I wonder if she ever told Keith that because he didn't act scared at all. In fact, she helped raise his first child from his college years. I never wanted to think of trying my luck with my mother. I just wanted to make her proud of me. She continued, "But shortly after I graduated high school, your father and I got married, and I joined the church. As a family, we got involved and began to live a strict moral lifestyle."

I hesitantly asked, "When did you have a miscarriage?"

"...after Keith and before you."

Her speech slowed down tremendously. "During the time your father and I were living together, I got pregnant again. I had become extremely stressed by the ridicule from church people that I didn't make it beyond seven weeks."

I could feel my mother's sorrow, and that was over forty years ago. I guess you never forget...we only learn how to cope. "I am sorry, Ma."

My mother looked at me with love. "You're going to be okay, baby. God gave me you, and I have never been so proud to be your mother."

"Aww, that means a lot, Mom."

"Seriously, baby. When you learn better, you do better. We all are just doing the best we know-how. That's why we should always pray that God shows us the path for our life."

Vea was right. Our parents were hands-on learners: they learned as they lived. Through her combined experiences with her mother, Grandma Evelyn, her sisters, teachers, and friends, my mother taught me. In fact, aren't we all doing the same thing as we maneuver through life?

"Mom, how did you get over your miscarriage? Mine still bothers me, and it is getting harder to live a chaste life."

"As far as my miscarriage, I will always remember August 15th. I was driving home from work and started cramping really badly. When I got home, I realized that I was also bleeding. I called your father, and he rushed home from work to take me to the hospital. I remember just crying as they rolled me to the ultrasound room and became embarrassed after finding out where the tech had to put the ultrasound probe. There was an excessive amount of blood, but your father held my hand as we both watched the screen and asked all too many questions that only the doctor could answer. After getting the results, he apologetically sent us home to let nature take its course. Unlike you, my fetus didn't pass, and I had to go back and have a D and C procedure. I am blessed to have had your father by my side."

I sat there fighting back the tears as I realized her tactics saved me from having a baby during my teenage years, but it didn't stop the shared experience that now created an unbreakable bond. It all made sense because my mother never left my side during my miscarriage. She didn't dish out any judgment toward me. Instead, she just loved me back on my feet.

"You know, Remi. I always wonder if it was a girl or a boy. I was secretly hoping for a girl, even though I would have been happy with either. But, then, you came along two years later, and I felt like God brought my baby girl back to me."

"What if that never happens for me, Mama? What if I never get married or have another child?"

The Hoover Dam released a river of my tears as I flopped faced down on Mama's bed. Mama began rubbing my back as my cry seemed to have come from my belly.

"Let it out. It's all right to let it out."

My cry had become whimpers until there was total silence. Then in good-ole mama fashion, the silence was broken; she turned me back to God because she knew she didn't have the answers.

"God knows your desires. God knows your heart, and God knows your pain. You will heal. He will give you an understanding of your pain and show you the path for your life. Baby, I don't have the answers, but you will find the peace you are seeking if you search deep within.
Nobody's perfect, Remi, and you know that. God knows that, and He has paid for our sins. He is not looking for perfection out of you. But rather a perfect heart, and baby, I don't know anybody that wants to do everything right more than you."

She was slick trying to throw a joke in, but she wasn't lying. I was a perfectionist, to say the least. Keith used to tease me about crying if I didn't make all A's on my report card when he was happy to have nothing below a 'C'. I released a smile to ensure Mama that her words didn't fall on deaf ears and that I was on the path to finding my peace.

Convictions

It was a drive to get back to my side of town, and my thoughts traveled faster than my car. I had a weekend with all of my girls...Vea, Aunt Cindy, Aja, Toi, Shay, and Mama. But one thing my Mama said stuck with me, we should always pray and allow God to show us the path for our lives. I needed to implement this from the beginning because people will judge you whether you are right or wrong. But the only real judge is God. So, in the silence of the night, I begin to talk to Him.

"God, I was introduced to you at a very young age. Even though I know that You are a loving God, I realize I have gotten to know you through a standard of keeping laws. I have spent over thirty years of my life trying to dot every 'I' and cross every 'T' to prevent from disappointing those I love while trying to keep your commandments presented by those who spoke Your word. In doing so, my peace has been shackled, and I am lost. I have learned that even though a group of people can all believe in an overarching principle, not all of them have the same convictions. Every animal you created, you created them to procreate. When you created a mate for Adam, you told them to be fruitful and multiply. Were they married in Your eyes or partnered to take care of their offspring like lions, tigers, and bears?"

I looked at the car monitor as a call had interrupted my conversation with God. It was my cousin, Bethany. I heard she moved to Peachtree City... no Newnan about a year ago. That's was a considerable distance from Buckhead, but I still planned to link up with her. I would call her later to set up a dinner date. But I needed to finish the current conversation, so I quickly declined the call with the message I can't talk now and changed my ringtone volume to silent.

Picking up where I left off, "God, I know sex was such a fundamental concept from the beginning. Why is it now being used to condemn us from doing what every animal does? The problem we are facing in the world is that some of us don't even have partners, yet we are burning with the natural passions of creation. Should my life be a constant fight with my own flesh regarding the natural course of life? Please show me the path of life for me. Because clearly, it is not like my grandmother who got married at thirteen or my mother, who was married at nineteen. It is not like my brother Keith who is now married and has a family, or like Auntie Cindy because I want a happy marriage. Even though cousin Shay provides a good representation of life, is that my life path? Show me God, the way of life for dealing with my flesh at the age of thirty-five. It is not like my friend Vea because I am not into self-pleasure, nor my soror Aja who keeps her a maintenance man. Well, just maybe, my path has resembled hers a time or too." I laughed, thinking I was more like Aja than I wanted to admit.

"Okay, for real, God, it is not Toi because I am not in denial. At the end of the day, I want to live with personal convictions inspired by you." In the silence and rhythm of the vehicle, with thirty minutes left of my drive, I focused on listening to a still and quiet voice. I was reminded that life is about what's in the heart, and it describes the real motive of our actions. Our convictions should be birthed from a personal relationship with our Creator, who gives much grace.

"God, Thank you for your grace and my journey to learn through my experiences about the birds and the bees."

Words from the Author & Editor

Praying for those who have experienced the loss of little ones playing in heaven. May the Creator of all send a spirit of comfort and peace within, knowing that HE has His reasons. We are left to feel the pain of loss, but we must find the purpose for our little ones who graced us with their presence.

May your experiences give you the tools of enlightenment for your ultimate walk with God, as Remi prayed in her talk with God. Our lives become powerful when we use the tools God has given us through our experiences. Likewise, our wisdom obtained from The Creator of ALL through our trials of life gives guidance and meaning to our greater purpose. So, continue to seek HIS path for your life journey.

God is with you.

About the Author

SANDREKA WAS BORN AND raised in Chambers County, Alabama, with two incredible parents, one sibling, and a host of supportive family and friends. She is a graduate of the University of Alabama at Birmingham, LaGrange College, and Jacksonville State University. She draws upon the interest of religion, life, and relationships to fuel her creative writing. Sandreka Y. Brown is a national board-certified mathematics teacher who also enjoys writing. In 2015, she became a published author with her teacher devotionals. She transitioned to writing fiction short stories and released her first story, Recycled Love, in March 2017. In 2019 she released her sixth publication and her first novel Love Bethany. The Birds and the Bees is her second novel and 7th publication.